T0063383

PRICE
OF
FREEDOM

MERRILL PHILLIPS

Order this book online at www.trafford.com
or email orders@trafford.com

Most Trafford titles are also available at major online book retailers.

Printed in the United States of America.

ISBN: 978-1-4907-1322-9 (sc)
ISBN: 978-1-4907-1321-2 (e)

Trafford rev. 09/23/2013

 www.trafford.com

North America & international
toll-free: 1 888 232 4444 (USA & Canada)
fax: 812 355 4082

ACKNOWLEDGMENTS

I wish to thank my grandson, Bryan Keller, for helping me with my new book. PRICE OF FREEDOM. He like myself is a veteran and understand what the service men and women have gone through to maintain the freedoms that we in America enjoy. He served with honor in the Marines. Bryan comes from a family of Marines, both his father and mother served in the Marine Corp. He now co-owns a flower shop in Brandon, Ms. called MUMS THE WORD.

CONTENTS

A HALLOWED PLACE

I was once a robust, healthy man, looking forward to
marriage and the raising of a family.

Then came this madman who thought that he could
conquer the world.

I volunteered to fight for and protect my country at
all costs.

Too many of my comrades paid the ultimate price,
they now lay at rest in our National Cemeteries.

Waiting for the day when the Lord will call them to
come forth from their graves.

Come forth they will, this time they will be whole
and free from the wounds of battle.

No longer will their flesh be torn by the shrapnel
that filled the air.

No longer will their bodies be feverish from the
wounds that they suffered at the hands
of their enemies.

Their eyes will no longer witness the death of
their fellow comrades.

They will no longer limp from the loss of a leg and
they will be able to reach out with that arm
that was severed by the bullets from hell.

The blind will once again see the rising and setting
sun and feel the warmth upon their flesh.

Their hearts will no longer grieve for their comrades,
who passed on before them, who never had the
chance to know the love of a wife or to
hold a child upon their knee.

At the return of the Lord our bodies will once
again be whole and full of the love
of the Lord.

No longer will we hate and try to kill
our fellow man.

Instead, we will stand before the lord and humble
ourselves in His presence, praising His name.

Asking for forgiveness for the deaths, we caused while
serving our country in its times of need.

Peace will once again reign in this war torn world when the Lord returns and He begins His reign of love.

Come quickly O Lord, we patiently await your return.

A SALUTE TO OUR FALLEN
COMRADES IN ARMS

To the ones who never came home, the ones who gave their all so the rest of us might remain free to live and worship God as we please. We salute you and your courage to face our enemies on the battlefields of the world and died so that the rest of us could live in freedom. You hesitated not when it came to going ashore on those foreign lands, well knowing that you might not return. You faced our adversaries square in the eye and knew that you had no choice but to kill your fellowman before he killed you. A hard choice to make but you made it out of loyalty to the families and friends you left behind. You knew that in order to return home you had to do what you were trained to do. It was a time for all to come to the aid of their country, you just happen to be one among many who would die so that the rest of us could live.

Many had reservations about pulling the trigger and killing those that they did not even know, but once that first shot was fired all things became fair, for in war it is kill or be killed, although this did not make it any easier to do. The biggest difference between the opposing forces was the uniform that they wore and the language they spoke. Put civilian clothes on them and let them stand side-by-side and one would be hard pressed to tell them apart.

I am very thankful that I did not serve in a combat role. I remember all too well the Hospital Planes that landed at our base in Newfoundland on the way back to the states with the most seriously wounded on board. I remember the smell of rotting flesh, burned flesh and the sight of the men with no arms or legs lying helplessly in their stretchers. At times, I can still smell that rotting and burned flesh; it had a smell that will remain with me the rest of my life. As bad, as this was you knew that combat must have been a living hell.

The young men of those years who had wives, girlfriends and plans for their future had no choice of what their future held. Either they were drafted or they volunteered to join the armed forces. The only difference being those who volunteered had a better chance of serving in the service of their choice. Once signed up they served for the duration of the war plus six months.

Most veterans served their country well and deserve their countries thanks and gratitude. Too many laid down their lives on foreign soil in places where we could not even pronounce the name, let alone where it was. These are the ones we salute for their ultimate sacrifice, for they not only gave their life, they also gave up their right to marry, raise a family and live in a country free from war so that their country might remain free. Many came back from war maimed and suffered the results of their wounds the rest of their lives, these too will be forever remembered by their comrades in arms and honored for their sacrifices.

The air war and the sea war was looked upon as being a clean war in the respect if your plane was shot down, it fell from the sky and left the sky clean. If your ship was sunk or you died at sea, you just disappeared beneath the waves and you or your ship was seen no more, thus leaving the surface of the sea clean. Whereas if the Dog-faced soldier who was killed or wounded laid on the battlefield until they were either cared for medically or buried, this could takes days and the carnage of battle was strewn everywhere, a reminder of the sacrifices of those involved. A dirty war with all of its scares, compared to the unseen scars of air and naval battles.

The civilian population of the en-battled nations took a terrible loss in both lives and destruction of their cities and towns. They were often caught in the middle of mortal combat with no place to hide and suffered much loss of life. Their place of employment and homes were destroyed, leaving many destitute, living off whatever they could find to sustain themselves. Many of their women raped to satisfy the lust of the prevailing armed forces. War invades the privacy of all involved and creates chaos that leads to the decimation of both personal and national agendas.

Had our enemies fully realized just how bad the United States was after the attack on Pearl Harbor they would have invaded our shores and possibly defeated us before we could stop them? Instead, it galvanized our country and brought us together as a people who would not stop until final victory. Just as many stories of heroism and sacrifice can be told of the American people as have been told of its fighting forces. We as a nation out produced and out fought our foes and in four years achieved a successful conclusion to WWII.

It took the consorted effort of both civilian forces and military forces to bring about the freedom that was realized after WWII. Though many wars have been fought since WWII, none has brought about as much patriotism as that one did.

My hometown lost three brave souls who gave their lives so that the rest of us could live in freedom. Robert Buck, Roland James and Scott Brown never lived to enjoy the freedom that they gave their lives for. They will live in the hearts and memories of those who knew them and be honored by those who served with them. As a nation we owe all of our fallen servicemen and women who gave their lives so that the rest of us might live free a debt of gratitude that can only be repaid by seeing to it that those who gave their all did not do so in vain.

A TRIBUTE TO ALL VETERANS

From 1775 to the present day all veterans who put life on hold and joined their comrades in defending this great nation are to be held in the highest esteem. The veterans of today and yesterday left family; friends, loved ones and their spouse and children so that they could defend our American way of life. After returning home, many are still fighting battles, but this time it is a fight to regain their place in society.

In all wars, many of these brave souls gave their all and never returned to society to take their rightful place in the town or city they left behind. They were looked upon as some kind of monster who went to war to kill and maim their opposing forces. They were shunned and made to feel that they were the ones who were responsible for the war that they fought in and suffered.

Too many still lie where they were killed and their remains are forever a part of the soil where they fell. Many of these brave souls will forever be just a note in history books, without name or nationality. Men and women on both sides gave their lives to defend what they perceived to be their way of life. Not until the day that all sides come together in peace will there be an end to the slaughter of the young people of the world.

In this country we celebrate the different wars by joining hands in appreciation and honoring the ones who never came home as a vibrant young person they were when they answered their call to defend the cause of freedom, not only in this country but also in lands with names that they could never pronounce. Veteran cemeteries all around the globe are filled with the remains of way too many young people from both sides of the conflict.

We who served and came home to a hero's welcome still remember those who died in our place. With heavy hearts, we will never be able to repay these men and women for their sacrifices without shedding tears. Tears that express our gratitude for the sacrifices they made so that we could live. At times, it is overwhelming to remember those who died for their country and were robbed of the opportunity to marry and raise a family. Too many generations have been lost to the ravages of war, generations that can never be replaced. It is the world's loss, for they would have become the backbone of our society and attributed to the welfare of their homeland.

For those who came home and were shunned, we the veterans of precious wars salute you and honor your service to our nation. These veterans were victims of a political conflict more than a war to restore peace and harmony. If those same politicians had to have served as grunts, there would not have been a war to start with. In one way or another all wars have had their roots in some political situation where one politician or another refused to be compassionate towards their counterpart.

They remained safe while they ordered their young men and women to take up arms and lay their lives on the line for their respective country.

From time immemorial, men and women have fought wars not of their making and have died for the cause of freedom. America has been the champion of freedom for all oppressed people regardless of their nationality. Freedom comes with a price, unfortunately too many have given their life so that the rest of us can live in and enjoy the freedoms that we have today. It is incumbent upon those who enjoy freedom to keep the fires of freedom burning by relating to coming generations what the price of freedom can and does require.

Only those who have served and sacrificed for the cause of freedom can fully appreciate what the price of freedom entails. It is more than waging a war. It is the willingness to put one's life on hold, take up arms, and die if necessary so that those left behind can remain free to form or maintain a government that will keep the peoples sacred right to govern themselves through a democratic process. A process where the people tell the government how they want to be governed rather than the government telling the people how they shall live.

Hold the banner of freedom high and stand behind those who serve in the armed forces and support them in whatever way is necessary when they return from battle. When you meet them on the street, give them a gesture of appreciation, just the nod of your head if nothing else. Former warriors do not want pity; they want to know the sacrifices they made on behalf of their country were not in vain. They will be the first to relegate all honors to those who never came home, whose lives were cut short and now lie in cemeteries around the globe.

Raise the Red, White and Blue, come together as a unified nation and honor all veterans from all of our wars by acknowledging their sacrifices and support those still living when they are in need. They gave (some their lives) so that their beloved country could remain free. Is it too much to ask to honor all veterans so that as individuals we can enjoy the freedoms that they fought and died for? I think not!

AMERICA THE BEAUTIFUL

A—America, the United States of America has the greatest example of democracy in the world.

M—Many times America has been attacked both militarily and economically and has prevailed. Once victorious America has been the leader in rebuilding its previous enemies inter-structure.

E—Every generation of Americans has produced those who have had the courage to stand against those who would, if they had their way, destroy our way of governing ourselves.

R—Ready to defend ourselves against all aggression, both domestic and foreign, this has kept America free. As a nation, we may argue and squabble among ourselves, but let a foreign power try to take advantage of it and we come together as a united people and defend ourselves.

I—International strife often causes turmoil in America, especially during election times. Foreign interests sometimes influence who thinks who the better candidate is. In the end, the candidate who puts the public's interest first comes out the winner. If they refuse to listen to their constituency, they generally serve but one term.

C—Coming from all nations America has become the most diverse nation the world has ever seen. It is this diversity of people who are seeking the freedom that makes America so great. Combined ideas of old country and a new beginning makes a difference in how America works and operates.

A—All through the history of America individual efforts has contributed to the greatness of our country. God has had His guiding hand on our nation and as long as we as a nation acknowledge God as the basic premise upon which this nation was founded we, as a nation will continue to be blessed among all nations. America is great, but greater yet is the word of God upon which America was founded.

T—Time will tell how long a nation formed by the desire to be free from a totalitarian government will survive. As long as we as a nation hold fast to the wishes and wisdom of our founding Fathers and their desires for America we as a nation will last until the second coming of our Lord and Savior, Jesus Christ. It is only through their efforts that we of today can enjoy the freedom that they have passed on to each succeeding generation.

H—Hold fast to Godly principles and the constitution and the United States of America will continue to be as a city set on top of a hill with its lights of freedom shinning for the entire world to see. It will continue to hold out its hand to all who wish to live under our way of life and support our freedom at all costs.

E—Every day give thanks to God for living in a nation where just one voice can make a difference as to how we live our lives and govern ourselves. This is one of the ways that makes America so great.

B—Better to live free and govern ourselves than to live under an oppressive form of government where just one person dictates how people live and work. Our veterans have sacrificed (some with their lives) so that the rest of us can live as a free people. To them we owe much.

E—Every person in the United States of America has a vote in how we govern ourselves. Those politicians who think that they know what is best for their constituents without their consent will find themselves looking for a new way of making a living. It is we the people who put them into office and it is we the people who can remove them from office. Our government officials are elected to serve the people, not the other way around.

A—Although we live in a free nation we must be vigilant in protecting our heritage of freedom. Many nations are not as fortunate as we are, for they face oppression of their freedoms every day of their lives. Never take your freedoms for granted.

U—Understanding what our ancestors went through to establish this great nation goes a long way in realizing that we of today have the responsibility of continuing the effort to protect our freedoms as our ancestors did. This includes giving our lives in defense of our freedoms.

T—This country gives everyone the opportunity to become whatever he or she wants to be. As a nation, we can accomplish whatever we set out to do. Against all odds in World War II, the United States of America came together as a nation and defeated those who thought they could defeat us militarily. We arose as one and everybody sacrificed for the good of all. A shining moment in the history of the United States of America where its entire population worked for the common good.

I—Initially the United States of America started out as a rag tag nation until today America is the most powerful nation in the world. To live as a free nation requires that its citizenry be willing to sacrifice for the common good, to stand shoulder to shoulder and say, "Thus far and no further." Be proud that in times of peril we as a nation put self-aside and work for the common good.

F—Fulfilling ones personal dream in life strengthens this nation we call America. This is the land where anyone can fulfill their dreams by working hard and complying with the laws that govern their personal pursuit.

U—Unless we as a nation allow God to be our inspiration to be an example for other nations we will have not fulfilled our full potential. This includes allowing anyone who wishes to better him or herself not to be held back by over regulation. After all our ancestors had a free hand in how they went about building this great nation. Therefore, we of today should not be held back by some Politian who does not think as we might.

L—Looking to the future, the United States of America has the potential to be a world leader by example rather than by force. We as a nation can either be great or fade into history as being just a mediocre nation. It is up to each of us to see to it that the United States of America remains a humanitarian nation. One who willingly reaches out to other nations who wish to emulate our ways of personal freedom?

God has blessed the United States of America from our very beginning and He will continue to do so in the future if we put Him first in our decision making process. America is beautiful, in its both citizenry and diversification of its population.

AMERICA, A NATION UNDER GOD

This nation was founded upon the proposition that all people are created equal and have the right to govern themselves. On this premise, we are equal in the eyes of God. We have the right to choose how we want to live, as a barbaric people or as a compassionate people where it is the duty of every citizen to be a friend and confidant to their neighbor, regardless of their color or status in life.

Our forefathers sacrificed their time, energy and fortunes to establish this nation as a free state, beholding to no other nation to help or guide it in the process of establishing a nation where all citizen may have a say in how they are to be governed. No other nation in the world has had such a meager beginning and grown to be the most influential and powerful nation the world has ever witnessed.

Without the foundation of the Scriptures to guide our forefathers this nation would not have the blessings of God to go ahead and form a society that through a common desire that all men are equal. Therefore, we of today owe our forefathers a debt of gratitude that can only be repaid by upholding the founding principles that they established in forming a democratic form of government.

During the founding of this nation there was opposition to the founding fathers who wanted to be governed by a king who would sit on his throne and govern by decree rather than by the consent of the governed. If they had had their way, we of today would be governed by the whims of one rather than by the consensus of the general population. Kings have come and gone, dictators have come and gone and through them and by them their subjects were suppressed and governed by whims that are contrary to the teachings of the Holy Scriptures and those they governed. No nation has remained free under such a form of government nor have they endured the test of time.

A free democratic nation, governed by the wishes of its people shall long endure as long as those who govern listen to the people and live by the founding fathers inherent belief in a God who will bless those who turn to Him for guidance in making laws by which to govern. When a nation turns their back of God and governs without regard for the populace then that nation is on the threshold of becoming a nation on the verge of collapse, for no nation in the history of man has survived for long without turning to God for guidance. Suppressed people will one-day rise up against a dictatorial form of government and either bring that form of government down or die in their efforts as witnessed in many parts of the world today.

The people of the United States of America have been blessed for founding a nation and government founded upon godly principles with the backing of its citizenry. We have struggled over the years to maintain our form of government and fought wars to preserve our way of life and have prevailed in our efforts. Unfortunately, today our government is being tried to its upmost by corruption that has infiltrated the highest positions in the land and if not reigned in will contribute to this nations down fall, for no nation can deny God by governing by decree rather than by the consent of the governed and survive. Washington D. C. has become a den of corruption unequaled in our history. When the different departments of our government fight among themselves and blame others for their mistakes then this nation is on a downward spiral with only one predictable end, the end of our nation as it was founded so many years ago.

Pray that the people of our nation rise up with one voice and demand change in Washington D.C. Demanding that our leaders return to the founding fathers faith in God and put the best interest of the people before their own pocketbooks and their own desires to rule to suit themselves rather than what the nation as a whole wants. That is to have a government that is governed by the consent of the people rather than by the dictates of a president who is putting undo hardships on the governed and generations yet unborn who will be burdened with unprecedented deficits. To govern by decree is but the first step in the downfall of this great nation. Under the founding fathers, no one person has the authority to suppress the consent of the people to advance their own agenda.

Our struggle to remain a free nation governed by the people and for the people as established by the constitution is in jeopardy, but by that same constitution, we as a nation hold elections by which we have the opportunity to either accept a candidate for public office or reject that candidate. It is therefore imperative that the public as a whole exercises that duty and votes for the best for the nation rather than by political party. Think about the best for our nation rather than by what some politician offers, question their ability to uphold the constitution over their personal desires. Inform yourselves about the issues; do not blindly follow one candidate over another just because he or she is of the same party as you are. Do not fall into the trap just because you may or may not receive government help in sustaining your way of life, that you will gain more by voting for the candidate who offers something for nothing. This is tantamount to becoming a form of bribery, one punishable by the law of the land, but unfortunately, today it is accepted as a way of life.

There is a lot riding on the outcome of the next election. The future of our country is at stake. Get or find a copy of our constitution, read it, read comments of our founding fathers and how they gave of their own fortunes to establish this nation. Their sacrifices are what this nation is based upon; they gave so that we of today might have liberty and the freedom to govern ourselves. Do not blindly relegate that responsibility to the politicians in Washington D. C . . . Stand up for your rights as a citizen of the United States of America and be a part in the affairs of our nation. We as individuals make up this great nation; do not be complacent and lose what so many veterans have died for. They died so that we as a nation and as individuals may enjoy the freedoms we have today.

Slowly but surely we are losing our freedoms through over governing by the politicians in our nation's capital. You and I can change that by electing officials who represent our desires rather than their own. We (you and I) are responsible for the future of this nation, therefore it behooves each one of us to become informed and vote on the premise that our founding fathers knew what they were doing when they established this nation. A nation for the people and by the people and that the government is responsible to the people who elect them, not some special interest group who only care more about their own agenda than the best interest of the nation.

Support the constitution of the United States of America. Support what it stands for. Look beyond self and work for the good of all Americans. Uphold the standards set by our founding fathers, encourage others to stand for the freedom to govern ourselves. Let politicians know that they are responsible to the people rather than the party they represent, for it is we the people who holds the power to govern not the politician. Keep God in our government and turn in Him when it comes to the affairs of our nation and we will be the nation that God wants us to be.

FREEDOM TREE

The tree of freedom that lines the pathway to our veterans cemeteries are strong and rooted deep in the ideal that our fighting forces are the greatest fighting men the world has ever seen. They ask not what or why, they just say, "Yes sir" and off to war they go. When faced with odds that would overwhelm most men they just keep on marching on towards victory. Even though many will give their lives on such missions, they quibble not and keep on marching.

Faced with decisions every day they wouldn't ordinarily make, but in times of war the soldier is well prepared to carry out their duty and assume the responsibilities that can either put their men in danger or turn aside. If the one in command can no longer continue with their mission, there is another who will step forward and takes command until the mission is completed. This is the kind of soldier that puts the welfare of his nation before self and does his best to complete his assignment.

We on the home front read of such men and wonder why they do what they do? Is it because they have no choice, I don't think so. I believe it is because they have a love for their country that surpasses their own safety and are willing to give their lives in the preservation of freedom in a land where from its conception men have stepped forward and defended this great nation when it has been threatened from without or from within.

Those who have never served this nation in times of war have no idea of the dangers that our fighting forces face on a daily basis. Of course, we sympathize with them and at the same time far too often, we criticize them for making mistakes that may have caused the death of innocent people. It is easy to assume such conclusions and put blame on the ones, who put their lives on the line every day,

The tree of freedom grows stronger every time our armed forces are asked to put their lives on the line so that we the public can live in a nation where serving our country in its time of need has become a tradition from its conception. It is these men and women whom we honor every year that so richly deserve our gratitude, for many never had the chance to know what it is like to marry and raise a family. Too many died way too young, but if asked to do it again they would be the first to step forward and fight for the freedoms that we enjoy today.

Let not the rabble-rousers regardless of who they are deter you from honoring the memories of those who gave their all so that we the living can live in a nation where freedom is a privilege and revered as a God given gift to all people, regardless of where they might live. Let the voices of our fallen comrades give you courage to stand up and pay tribute to those who now lie silent in their graves. Silent they may be, but listen closely and you will hear their whispers on the winds of time encouraging we the living to stand fast in freedom and water the freedom tree with whatever it will take to maintain the freedoms that they gave their lives for.

Be proud of these men and women who lie in our cemeteries under the shade of the freedom tree. Let not their memories be tarnished or their deeds of valor go unappreciated, for with them lies the roots that nourish the freedom tree and gives vitality and life to this great nation. Without the sacrifices of these noble men and women, we of today would be talking a different language and saluting a different flag.

ONWARD THEY MARCHED

While attending a military funeral I witnessed a marvelous sight. The stars and stripes were flying at half-mast, strains of our national anthem filled my ears and as I gazed skyward I saw a standing army as if marching off to war.

They no longer looked at one other across a field of battle or sniped at one another from concealment; they were now brothers in arms marching as a unified army towards an unseen foe.

With full field dress, they marched across the sky, some in the uniforms of old and marching to the fife and drum, others to the cadence of our national anthem and even others to the music of foreign lands.

It was a sight to see; fighting men from all of the armies of the world marching together with their banners going on before, could it be that I was witnessing an end-time event where all of the armies of the past, present and future were marching to fight the final battle between good and evil?

This I know not, but there they were, marching in harmony across the sky. From all the lands, young and old alike now were marching to a different tune. Men who had left family, friends and sweethearts behind and had said their farewells were now carrying the hope of the world that they would triumph over evil.

Through the ringing in my ears as the honor-guard fired a twenty one-gun salute to honor their fallen comrade I heard a voice from heaven declare, "This army that you see marching across the sky is of God and it is preparing for battle at Armageddon. There they will be tested and found to be true. For in the end the army of God shall prevail over evil and you on earth shall live in peace forever and ever."

This standing army seemed to march on forever, there seemed to be no end. Every now and then, there was a break in their ranks and in these breaks were flag bearers. These flag bearers were carrying the banner of the cross. With honor, they marched with eyes gazing beyond the horizon as if being guided by an unseen hand.

Remembering the teaching of the past, I recalled the scriptures that declared that there would be one last battle between good and evil, that it would be in a place called Armageddon, and that the marching army that I saw in the sky would triumph over evil.

As the military funeral concluded I once again gazed skyward, the marching army I saw in the sky had faded away, and only the sun shone behind two clouds and reflected off the cross on the grave of this warrior who had gone on to join that army in the sky.

SIDE BY SIDE

In veteran cemeteries around the world, they lay side by
side, row upon row they lay in silence in mute
testimony of wars gone by.

Their footsteps are silenced upon the battlefields of the
world, no longer heard as they march to
a different drumbeat in a new place
and a new time.

Walking among the grave markers, I hear their tales of
adventure upon the gentle breezes as they
rustle through the distant trees.

Telling the stories of how GI Joe met his demise as he
was defending his country in a land far
from home.

Merrill Phillips

It is with a humble heart that I stand in silence and
salute my fallen comrades as one by one
they gave up life and bowed to
the grim reaper.

No longer do they march as a strong and proud soldier,
sailor, marine, or airman, they march as proven
men of valor to a different tune.

No longer do they feel the sting of death as when that
bullet pierced their body and felt the pain
before opening their eyes in eternity.

Out of reverence I kneel before their graves and bow my
head in prayer, petitioning God to console these
brave souls when through the door of death
they marched.

Both friend and foe alike suffered great losses, now they
all stand side by side embracing the creator of all.

Seeking God to alleviate the pain and suffering of the world,
that peace might be unto all nations so that their
fellow comrades will not have to suffer the
rigors of war.

In silence they may lie but their heroic deeds and sacrifices
will hopefully inspire generations to come to do all to
avoid armed conflict and the loss of life.

Wars take away the lifeblood of a nation; generations are lost
when just one brave soul lays their life down for
the good of all.

It is for we the living to come together and pay tribute to the
ones who without fear and trepidation gave their all so
that the rest of us can live in a nation where
freedom prevails.

SURVIVAL AGAINST ALL ODDS

As I stood overlooking the open field in front of me, I saw the advancing line of men who seemed to be under the spell of not knowing just what they were there for, with no intentions of killing or being killed. I could hear their Captain hollering orders to advance, without hesitation they moved forward with guns pointing towards us. Then our orders came to advance and I felt like running in the opposite direction to the safety of home. My feet kept moving in the direction of the foe, but my heart was far from this field of death.

As we advanced, the crack of rifle fire filled my ears and distant puffs of smoke from the enemy's line told me that death was near, but the excitement of the moment kept me going. Then the cannons opened fire and clouds of dust rose from the earth and I could hear the cries of death emerging from the smoke of the exploding shells. Both we and they were being blown into eternity, pieces of bodies lying everywhere, an arm here, a foot without a shoe there, Yanks and Rebels groaning from gaping wounds and the dead who will never see home again. Just as I reached out to help the one next to me, he fell to the ground and stirred no more.

There was not time for fear, not even time to be afraid, just keep moving and firing at unseen souls ahead of us and they in turn did the same. Men from both sides were falling from the barrage of bullets that sounded like bees as they sped on their way, delivering death to those in their way.

The cannon kept bellowing flame and smoke, their barrels too hot to touch, but fire on they did. As one loader dropped from the sting of death, another stepped forward to keep death belching from within. On it went for what seemed like an eternity, hesitating only long enough for another shell to be rammed down the throat of those roaring monsters of death.

I kept moving forward, stumbling over the dying and the dead, their battle was over, but mine kept going, I stopped only long enough to reload my rifle and send another piece of lead on its way to do its dastardly deed. I remember praying that my bullet would not find its mark, for the opposing forces did not want to die or be wounded any more than I did. The reason for this battle was not important now, just to take the nest step and not feel that piece of hot lead pierce my body, was all anyone could ask.

Soon we would be face to face with our foes and there would not be time to reload these muzzleloaders, then would come hand-to-hand combat. My eyes burned from the smoke of battle, I lost the taste of killing, I just wanted to survive this hell on earth and return to the peace of home. As I stumbled into a shell hole, I felt the blood of one of my fallen comrades as it soaked through my trouser leg. Then I looked up and saw a big, raw-boned Reb standing over me with the look of death in his eyes, his bayonet poised to run me through. At that same moment, I watched his face turn to one of pain and disbelief, His body went limp as he fell to the blood soaked ground. I rolled over onto my back and saw a friendly face smiling down at me. There was not time to say thanks, but the thought of why did this man have to die so that I could live ran through my mind.

Just as quick as the gunfire had started it stopped; the foe had had enough and was retreating. The stillness that followed brought the reality of what I had just gone through to the forefront of my mind. It was overwhelming with the dead and dying all around me and for whatever reason I did not even have a scratch on me. The smell of death filled the air, a smell that would stay with me the rest of my days. Two thousand men died that day; I would later recall that that smiling face was a face of an angel who in the midst of battle kept me from being among the dead. My hopes were that this fight between brothers would be over soon and that the survivors would learn to live in harmony.

THE FLAG OF FREEDOM

The flag that stands for freedom still flies high over
the land where it was conceived.

Despite its desecration by those who seek to destroy
it, it still unfurls in the breezes of freedom.

It has waved over the battlefields of the world and
rallied the troops of freedom on to victory.

It has draped the coffins of fallen comrades and
comforted the bereaved as their remains
were lowered into their graves.

The politicians shroud themselves in the stars and
stripes while seeking to woo you and me into
voting for them.

The stars and stripes stand for freedom no matter
where she waves.

Freedom seeking people flock to our shores where
she flies high and proud.

Never has she or will she ever hang her head in
shame or bow to the tyranny of
the Caesars' of the world.

She stands watch through the darkness of night
and greets the dawn of each new day with
the pride that comes with freedom.

People living under her protection represent the
different cultures of the world.

Cemented together by one common cause, freedom
for all who love and live by her laws.

Our forefathers were guided by God above when they
set forth to establish a nation where all, could
stand together as one.

Great this nation is and great it will be as long as it's
people rally together and wrap themselves
in the furls of Old Glory.

A flag that stands as a shining star in the midst of a
world that is shrouded in darkness and despair.

A nation fueled by the love of God and a flag that
represents freedom will always prevail as
long as she allows freedom for all,
not just a select few.

There is only one flag conceived in the spirit of freedom,
tested in battle and found to be worthy of its
name, **OLD GLORY,** long may she wave
over the home of the free and
the brave.

HALLOWED GROUND

As I enter this hallowed place, I can feel the presence
of those who have gone on before.

I watch the gravediggers on the side of the hill digging
the grave that will be the resting place of the next
one who will join those who are now at rest.

I walk from stone to stone reading the names and
remembering those whom I once knew.

Some were fishermen, painters, carpenters, plumbers,
sea Captains, daughters, mothers, grandmothers
and many other professions.

Some passed from old age, some from disease, and others
long before they had time to experience what
life had in store for them.

Small American flags mark the graves of those who served
their nation in times of war, never again to hear the cry
of the wounded and dying on the battlefields of
the world.

They all had one thing in common, they all lived and
played in the same community, living and
loving as they willed.

The faithful rest in peace while the lost served a different
god and now they have paid the price.

The older I get the more the names of old friends and family
that I lived and worked with are here among
the deceased.

All too soon, I will join them in this resting place that I now
roam.

As I leave this hallowed place, I turn
and watch the gravediggers
who will all too soon dig the grave where I will be put to rest.

FIELD OF STONES

With tears welling up in my eyes I gaze across this field of stones and remember the days I served my country, defending the freedom that my ancestors passed on to me and my generation.

Each stone represent a hearty soul who was called to the defense of their country in time of war, without thoughts of death; they stepped forward to defend their country in its time of need. Little did they realize that it might be they who would be called upon to lay down their life so that the rest of us could return home and live in freedom.

With a lifetime before them, they left home and family and joined the ranks of our fighting forces and defended our freedom wherever they were called to serve. Some served on land, some upon the open seas, some under the sea, and others in the air, but no matter where they served, they served with pride and never flinched when faced with insurmountable odds.

It was with pride that we of my generation put on our uniforms and marched off to war, a war not of our making but one we had thrust upon us and for this reason, we joined hands and formed the greatest fighting force ever assembled.

The price for defending our country was high in both lives and materials lost in some of the most fierce fighting ever encountered by any fighting force anywhere, for our common enemies were hell bent on destroying this nation and what it stands for.

With an inbred determination to remain free at all cost our fighting forces fought on to total victory under difficult circumstances, even when the odds of victory was against us we fought ever harder and refused to surrender when it would have been easier to do so and suffer what may.

Were it not for the thoughts of returning home in freedom many would have given up in despair and suffered the losses, but that spark of freedom came forth in full blaze to give them hope in victory.

Way too many died in the invasion of foreign lands. The sting of death was all around them and unfortunately, one of the bullets had their name on it. Their lose was felt throughout the ranks of their comrades and this gave them reason to fight on without regard for their own safety, but rather with a determination that they were fighting for freedom for themselves and all of the freedom loving of people of the world.

Slowly but surely the tide of war turned and our fighting forces prevailed over their enemies and they returned home in victory, battered and war weary they were mustered out of their units and took up their lives where they left off. Unfortunately, many carried the scars of battle to their dying days, some to never recover from the hell they faced on the field of battle.

Those of us who still live remember the days when life was measured from one battle to the next. We regret not our service to our country, but we do regret the loss of life that many of us witnessed on both sides of the conflict. Thousands on both sides joined their comrades in arms because they had no choice but to obey the order of the day, fight for your country and ask not the reason why.

Many of those whom we fought against have through the years become our friends that we would today defend to the death. All sides have their Fields of Stones and they like we honor their dead and pray that the warriors of the future will be able to settle their differences in the courts of arbitration where all sides can come to an amicable agreement.

A SOLDIERS PRAYER

O God, forgive me the death I deliver to my foes,
I pray that it were not so.

I prefer to have them as my friends, but they
refuse to come to the table of love.

The days are dreary, the nights long as the hell
of battle sounds all around and yet I find
peace whenever I pray to Thee.

The flash of cannon, the crack of the rifle fill the
air and keep me from sleep, finally weary and
tired I fall fast to sleep, resting in the
comfort that You will see me
through.

As the early morning, light breaks the eastern sky
I once again pray to You that this day will
bring peace and hope for tomorrow.

The stench of death fills the air, bombs bursting like
firecrackers on the fourth of July, shrapnel
piercing the bodies of my buddies and
yet death evades me.

Why am I spared the pain of death, the hole in my
helmet is testimony that God has His hand on
me and yet I know not why I am spared.

Perhaps it is proof that God has something else for
me to do when this war comes to an end, if so
I am ready to follow Him wherever He will
lead me.

As they say there are no atheists in foxholes, I am
beginning to believe that that is true, for a
friend of mine just before he died asked
if I would say a prayer for him.

I held his hand as life drained from his body, just
before he closed his eyes in death he looked
at me and said, "Do you see what I see?"
I turned to him and replied, "No, tell
me what you see".

With that he returned, "I see the Lord of heaven
holding out His hand to me. Him I cannot
refuse. Bless you my friend for praying
for me."

With that said my buddy closed his eyes in death,
to my amazement there was a smile on his
face, never more will he feel the sting
of death, for in the arms of the Lord
of heaven he now rests.

From within I felt the desire to pray, but the heat of
battle turned me away, even so I felt the Lord
of heaven had His hand on me and was
calling me to a higher calling, one
for now I did not understand.

The day did come when that war came to an end. I
returned home to a hero's welcome, but my
soul was not at peace.

I struggled to cope with the carnage of war and what
it had done to me, from alcohol and drugs I
found no relief.

This was a different war; this was a war for my soul.
Finally I gave up and turned to the Lord of
heaven and asked Him to come into my
life.

Behold, true to His word almighty God took me by
my hand and lead me to the altar of forgiveness,
there I was cleansed of feelings that had
become a barrier between Him
and me.

I now stand in a pulpit among the sheep and the wolves proclaiming the word of God and how He had changed a killing machine into a saint.

One worthy of the love of God, one willing to stand in the gap and proclaim the word of the Lord of the universe, my God and your God.

A-men

BASIC FREEDOMS

It is time that we as a nation stand up and protect
the freedoms that the veterans have fought
and died for.

Time to say an unequivocal NO to those who are
trying to change our way of life by denying
us our basic freedoms.

Such as freedom of speech, free to pray whenever
and wherever we feel the desire to do so.

Freedom to protect the un-born who are now being
murdered before they have a chance to live.

This nation will suffer greatly in the years to come
for such atrocities. To deny the right to live
is a travesty indeed.

No nation can survive that denies basic human rights,
history will bear this out.

Our veterans have fought and died all around the
world in an effort to support freedom.

Those who restrict freedom are in direct contrast to
what our veterans have made great sacrifices for.

It is little wonder that the youth of today do not
know how to react to what is going on around
them.

We as a nation are failing to set a proper example for
our youth to look up to.

Some groups of this great nation are trying to change
our basic way of life and in so doing are
undermining our Christian heritage.

Our forefathers established this nation on Christian
values based on the truths of God.

Today we are finding these values eroded away by
indifference and the lack of patriotism on
behalf of those who promote an
immoral society.

Think back to the days when this nation was in
peril of losing its freedom through war.

The danger brought us together as a nation that
would not tolerate any threat to our freedom
nor our way of life.

Unfortunately, today as a nation we do not hold to
the basic truths like we did during the time of
world war11.

At one time we stood head and shoulders above the
rest of the world as a nation that stood for
freedom for all its people.

Today many of our freedoms are in jeopardy of being
compromised because of the liberalism in our
judicial system that have granted special
privileges to those who want to
change our way of life.

They are passing laws that limit the activities of those
who are willing to stand up and fight for what is
right in the eyes of God. In fact the use of
the word "God" is limited by some of
the recently passed laws.

It may take another Hitler or Communistic government
to wake us up and bring us back to our roots
as a free nation.

Many are willing to fight and die for our basic rights rather
than to give in to every disgruntled sect that comes
along, instead of giving in to such groups as
we are doing today.

To remain free it is right that we should honor our veterans
and what they fought and died for, to come together
as a nation undivided in our basic freedoms as
set forth by our founding fathers.

Freedom under the auspices of God is the only freedom
that no matter how hard some groups might fight
to eliminate, cannot change. An edict set
forth by God supersedes any and
all efforts by man.

FREEDOM

Freedom comes with a price; it is not in this world automatic, although this was the intent of God.

We sacrifice much at times to remain free; too often, it is our lives.

From Flanders Field to the blue waters of the Pacific Ocean many a soul lies in a service member's grave.

From the coast of Maine to the Hawaiian shores, our youth have fought and died to keep our home front secure and free.

Those who have survived the carnage of war will say the same thing; "Freedom is for all, not just a select few."

F—Faithful prayer warriors pray for freedom for all people of the world.

R—Righteousness is the goal of all Christians, which produces real freedom.

E—Everyday offers opportunities to witness to others and promotes peace.

E—Equality is for all, only when one tries to dominate another does conflict and war arise.

D—Death of too many young men has come about by leaders who have a desire to dominate their neighbors.

O—Only when we as a people uphold the laws of God can we live in harmony with our fellowman.

M—Memorial Day is a day to remember and honor the dead who have given their lives on our behalf.

FREEDOM WORTH STRUGGLING FOR

As you wander throughout this great country observe the flag that flies high over this land of the free and the brave, its stripes denote the shedding of blood for the cause of freedom.

It was not always so, there was a time when the flag of the British Empire flew from every ship's mast and flagpole and we were governed from the throne of England.

The Red Coats marched to a different tune than we of today and kept us in order through the power of the king of England. They kept the embers of freedom from bursting into flame. Subdued, the colonist grumbled whenever the king leveled new taxes to keep his coffers full.

Under the flag of tyranny, the colonist strived to raise voices, but to no avail, every time the burden of taxes increased. Then came the day when enough was enough, their hearts afire for the taste of freedom, the colonist arose from the depths of oppression and declared with one voice, "NO MORE."

With this began our struggle for freedom, brave men and women gathered in secret and laid plans of rebellion against the king. Some hesitated to join them for fear of retaliation and heavier taxation. Regardless of the consequences, they went ahead with their plans, for the smoldering desire for freedom had come to full flame and there was no turning back.

From smoldering ashes came the flames of freedom, fanned by desperation, fed with thoughts of self-governing, the farmers and merchants formed a fighting force that would pave the way to a free nation, free from an oppressive government without representation.

In old Boston Town the bedraggled rebels started by throwing English tea into the harbor, from that act the struggle for freedom burst forth, some skirmishes lost, some won, others a draw, but the spirit of freedom could not be held back or put down.

Fighting broke out throughout the colony and the battle of Bunker Hill encouraged others to join the fight. The taste of freedom was everywhere and no one held back their support of establishing a government based on Biblical principles where the people would have a say in how they were to be governed.

Soon the rest of the colonies joined in the fight for freedom, come victory or defeat they had come too far to coward now. Many gave their lives for the freedom that burned deep within their souls. On they fought, sometimes never knowing whether the struggle would end in victory or defeat. One thing was clear; they either would triumph in victory or be buried beneath their beloved soil in death.

At long last, the tide turned in their favor and this in itself kept the fires of freedom burning ever brighter. Finally, the Red Coats had enough and they left our shores in defeat.

This young struggling nation was born and freed from oppression, like a horse that takes its bit in its teeth and runs unencumbered, so our nation was established as a viable nation, shaky at first, but as time passed it grew in strength and power and has remained free from foreign oppression ever since.

Many foreign powers have tried time and time again to squelch the taste of freedom, but our founding fathers placed this struggling nation under the authority of God's word and ever since it has stood as a "Light" before the whole world. A nation where the oppressed people of the world can come and taste the freedom brave souls of the past gave their lives for.

This nation shall endure as long as there are those who will stand up and give their lives so that those remaining can dwell in a land where freedom comes before self-interest. Freedom will always require sacrifice, but the rewards of freedom will and has brought out the best in all of us. Opposition to freedom may always be, but if we as a nation support freedom for all, freedom will never let us down.

May the stars and stripes fly forever over this great land that we call America and for what it stands for, a refuge from oppression, a nation where one can voice their opinion without the fear of retaliation.

Fight when we must, for freedom demands it, our longing for freedom encourages us as a nation to fight for freedom when necessary and to be compassionate towards those who are still struggling for what most of us would give our lives for.

Just ask any soldier of the past and they will tell you that even the thought of freedom is enough to encourage them to fight for freedom again if they had to and to lay down their life for freedom if necessary. God ordained freedom for all nations, but few there are who have achieved the freedoms that we of America enjoy.

Reaching out to foreign nations who have the desire to be free from oppression is the duty of all free nations, to do otherwise would take away from our own freedom, to coward before tyranny weakens us all.

Let the fires of freedom burn deep within your soul, giving you courage to stand up in the face of adversity and declare, "Freedom for all or no freedom at all". Let this be your motto and let it guide your thinking when someone asks, "Will you help me achieve the same freedom that you enjoy?"

FROM SHORE TO SHORE

From Concord, Massachusetts where the shot that was fired that was heard around the world to Bunker Hill the patriots who struck out against English taxation without representation started the process of seeking freedom that still goes on today. Though the weapons and locations have changed, the desire to live as a free nation still prevails.

There are hundreds of cemeteries around the world where our brave American fighting men and women have been laid to rest. Row upon row of grave markers in these cemeteries is overwhelming evidence of the price that we as a nation has paid for our freedom. There must be something special about a nation who's Sons and Daughters are willing to give their all so that the rest of us can enjoy our God given freedoms.

They never hid behind excuses or ran from their duties; they did what they did because of love and commitment to their country. They did not run and hide because they disagreed with their commanding officer, they might not have liked them, but they had respect for them and their position, They did as they were ordered to do. Many lost their lives obeying commands that put them in harm's way, go they did, not regretting their decisions.

These fallen heroes were the cream of our country, our pride and joy, full of the spirit of freedom. They represented all nationalities; they had a heritage and a lust for freedom and the democratic way in which we live.

Freedom is not freedom unless you are willing to fight and die for it if need be, willing to fight for it wherever it is threatened, whether it be domestic or foreign. The battlefields of the world have run red with American blood given in defense of our freedom and the freedom of our allies.

We as a nation need never hang our head in shame, many nations may despise us, but there is not one nation that does not know that the United States of America is but a sleeping giant and will spring to life if our freedoms are threatened. As a nation we have been tried by fire and found to be a worthy opponent, when necessary we will strike out against tyranny with or without the consent of our allies.

We are a free nation and will remain so as long as we have brave souls such as these who now sleep in our national cemeteries. They have done their duty and left us a legacy that we as a nation can be and are proud of. Freedom is like a smoldering fire, it will never go out, and when it is threatened, it will burst into flame and will prevail as long as we hold to our God given rights. If we stray from our God given rights, we will be in danger of losing our freedom, but as long as we hold the banner of God as we defend our freedom we shall prevail.

Dear God may theses brave souls who lie in the different cemeteries around the world rest in peace. May we as a nation never desecrate their resting places, may their souls be free from the bondage and desecration that surrounds us today, may they know the peace that goes with freedom. May the stars and stripes forever wave over their final resting place until the coming of our Lord and Master, Jesus Christ.

GENERATION TO GENERATION

God has blessed this land we call America, hold the torch of freedom high and let your support of our troops be known before the whole world.

As the clouds of war appear on the horizon turn to God and let Him guide and encourage us as a nation we face adversity.

Wars have come and gone and the flag that we hold in such high esteem still waves over the land that we call the home of the brave and the free.

Many of our youths have given their lives in the defense of this great nation; never let their dream of freedom fade, for by them and through them, we still live free.

From generation to generation our youth have passed the torch of freedom from one to the other, may it always be so. Though many of our youth may fall in battle they hold our future in their hands.

Support our fighting personal as our predecessors supported our generation as we fought and died in order to pass the flag of freedom to the next generation, thus proclaiming our resolve to remain free.

From the founding of this great nation to the present time, our youth has sustained the freedoms that we hold so dear, freedom that our predecessors passed on to us.

Hold the stars and stripes in high esteem, remember and be thankful that we still are a free nation where we can express ourselves as we do, freedom of expression is one of our greatest assets and will never fade as long as our youth step forward and protect it with their lives.

God certainly has had His hand on this nation and as long as we follow His leading, we will remain a free and productive nation, turn from God and follow our own initiatives will only bring disaster upon ourselves.

As a great nation, we have the obligation to reach out to the hurting people of this world and help them obtain the freedoms that we so often take for granted. To do otherwise is to refuse to recognize that they too deserve the chance to govern themselves as we do.

Through the grace of God, we as a nation are one of the most blessed nations that there has ever been, to hold these blessings without sharing them with others who are seeking freedom demeans our own.

With the spirit of God in our hearts, we have become a city set upon a hill with the torch of freedom shinning for the whole world to see. It is therefore our responsibility to support other nations that are going through what we have been through in our struggle for freedom.

As the youth of this nation has fought for our freedom over the generations we of the older generation know what it means to put our lives on hold while our nation struggled to preserve the freedom that was passed on to us. We did it out of love and duty to the generation that passed the flag of freedom to us and so may it be until the second coming of our Lord and Savior, Jesus Christ.

IN MEMORY OF OUR
FALLEN COMRADES

As we, go forth as a renewed nation dedicated to the proposition that all are created equal let us not forget what they did here.

We are here to commemorate those who have put forth their lives so that the rest of us might enjoy the fruits of freedom and see to it that they did not give their lives in vain.

Through the long struggle to retain our freedom the rest of us have foregone the creature comforts that we now can return to and enjoy to the fullest.

We as a nation owe these who we now commit to their final resting place a debt of gratitude that can never be fully paid.

They hesitated not to face the heat of battle so that you and I might avoid the onslaught of death and destruction.

Many committed acts of bravery that will never be known, for how else can one account for such big losses among those who tried to defeat the cause of freedom.

Through days and nights of hell, these brave souls stubbornly fought and prevailed against an enemy who had intentions of flying their flag over our sovereign land.

We here and now dedicate ourselves and our resources to the restoration of this great nation. Guided by the mighty hand of God we shall not fail.

Though these brave souls shall never again walk among us, they are now enjoying the fruits of their labor in the presence of God almighty.

This is the time of rededication to the fundamental God given freedoms that we hold so dear in our hearts.

Freedoms that our forefathers established when they prevailed against the tyranny of taxation without representation.

As they laid down their lives so that we could enjoy freedom so have these here done the same so that our children and grandchildren might live free from the burdens of war.

We are a nation of blessed people who will if necessary leave our homes and families and lay down our lives to keep from losing that which these dedicated men and women have died for.

In no way can these lives be replaced and no way can we as a nation allow the carnage of war destroy our way of life.

In the future we must seek ways to avoid such conflicts through negotiations without compromising our God given right to govern ourselves. No nation, great or small can offer what this great nation can offer its citizenry.

Though our form of government has many faults it is without a doubt the greatest form of government yet devised by the mind of man.

Therefore, be proud to live in a nation where all citizens have the right to voice their opinion and vote their conscience without threat of retribution.

May this nation long endure and stand as a model for the rest of the world to see and admire.

Through our representative form of government we can mold our nation into what we feel is in the best interest of the majority.

May our great flag fly high in the breezes of freedom and may it always fly over a nation that will honor its dead who have fought and died to keep us free.

May God guide us as individuals and as a nation and may His will be done in our lives as we resume a peaceful path with justice and freedom for all.

JUST PLAIN FOLKS

From the north, from the south, from shore to shore they came and formed a mighty army ready for battle.

They raised their banners high and marched to the cadence of the fife and drum.

They formed the greatest fighting force the world had ever seen.

They fought the invading hordes on the land, the sea, and in the air and drove them from their land.

When the sound of battle was over, they returned to their peaceful ways.

Every year they gather together to honor their fallen comrades.

Remembering when they had faced their enemies on the battlefields of the world and prevailed when all seemed to be lost.

Now they are old with memories of the days when they restored peace where there was no peace.

Bowing their heads in reverence to God and praising His holy name for seeing them through times of hell on earth.

Memories of battles and the cry of death fill their thoughts as tears flow without shame in reverence to those they left dead and dying on the field of battle where boys became men.

No longer do they fear death, for they conquered their fears when they looked their enemies in the eye, stood fast and prevailed.

They are now content to rest in the twilight of life and come together each year and renew old acquaintances.

One by one, they have succumbed to the trials of life and joined their comrades in arms in death. However, this time they have joined a new army, one that marches to the cadence of heavenly music with the cross of Jesus flying on before.

HOW MANY MORE

How many more of our young men and women have to die keeping our land free from oppression, O Lord? We pray that those who have made the supreme sacrifice will not have died in vain.

Those who have died so that we may remain a free nation represent the spirit of freedom.

Not only for us did they die, but for all of the freedom loving people the world around.

They left their families behind and ventured into the jaws of death with the hope of seeing the day when war will not be a part of their future.

As long as there are those who try to suppress freedom loving people and do not believe that Jesus Christ is the Son of God, then the youth of freedom seeking nations will have to do battle to keep them free.

May God have mercy on these un-repentant souls and may He touch their hearts so that they too might obtain eternal life, this is the desire of all Christians.

Unfortunately, as long as Satan remains prince of this world there will be conflict between the believers and the un-believers.

Final victory over oppression will not come to this sin-filled world until the return of Jesus Christ, and then He will cast Satan and his fallen angels into the bottomless pit. This will be a glorious day for all who hold the banner of freedom high, for then the task of defending freedom by means of war will have come to an end.

There will be peace on earth as God intended and the threat of war will be no more. The songs of freedom will be on the lips of all freedom loving people.

Their voices of praise will rise onto heaven and God will honor all who have given their lives in the pursuit of freedom from the days of Adam and Eve unto the present time.

The children of the future will have a glorious day in which to live, a day when the sound of war will be a thing of the past. Our youth will not have to face the devastation that we of today have to endure and we will not have to ask, "How many more will have to die in defense of freedom O Lord?"

MEMORIAL DAY

Flags line the way that leads to a soldier's grave, gentle breezes make them unfurl and reveal the beauty of the old Red, White, and Blue.

Each drop of blood that was shed upon the battlefields of the world is represented by the red stripes in our flag.

These brave souls who now rest in peace stepped forward to defend their native land, all too many died to keep us free.

Row upon row of crown-crested stones fills these fields among the trees; each stone signifying that here lays a service man or woman who freely gave their life so that the rest of us could live free.

From every state, they came and went to war not knowing if they would live or die, fight they did until a bullet from hell ended their life.

Those who survived have within their heart the memories of their comrades in arms who gave their all so that the rest of us might remain free. At times this is a heavy burden for them to bear and often ask, "Why them and not me?"

Old Glory still flies over us all, alive or dead, long may she wave and always be a symbol of freedom, fought and won by so many and enjoyed by so few.

We the living owe these brave souls more than we will ever be able to repay, our burdens are at times heavy to bear, but we can console ourselves in the knowledge that their deaths were not in vain.

Through tempest and storms, they marched against our foes and rose victorious over their fears of not coming home.

Those who stained foreign soil with their blood will themselves rise victorious over their own graves and rest in peace with their Creator.

Long may these flags wave over the graves of these immortal souls, wave on Old Glory, wave on.

May the day never be when Old Glory hangs her head in shame in the breezes of time, for too many have given their lives for this to be.

Wherever you see, Old Glory on display remember those who died so that you and I might remain free are observing us from their graves.

It is for us the living to keep their memories from fading from view and for us to see that they did not give their lives in vain.

Remember that it was these who now are deceased who stood as a standing army and fought for our freedom and shed their blood so that you and I might be free.

We are bound by heritage to these who now lie still in their graves; they gave their all so that we might be free. We in return owe them a debt of gratitude for stepping forth and defending freedom wherever the need.

May they rest in peace and forever be our legacy, may Old Glory forever wave over these graves, and may our memories always be how they gave their all for victory.

As they are now, so one day we must be. The day will come when all will meet beyond the grave and meet Jesus Christ face to face, until then may Old Glory wave over the land of the free and home of the brave.

LEST WE FORGET

O how still they lie, once vibrant, full of life, now they lie silent in their graves, from all walks of life they came, came together to form the greatest fighting force ever assembled.

When their country was attacked without provocation, they gathered from border to border and from shore to shore, standing shoulder to shoulder, they made an impressive sight indeed.

Through the rigors of basic training, they marched, readying themselves to face our foes on the battlefields of the world. With their heads high and their hearts full of pride, they marched to the cadence of a country at war.

Leaving families behind, kissing their sweethearts good-bye, they marched off to war, praying that the war would be short and that everyone would return home, but knowing in their hearts that many would give their lives for the cause that lie before them.

On the high seas they sailed, beneath the waves they sought out the enemy, in the skies above they flew and carried the fight to the homeland of their foes, they marched across hill and dale with the conviction that they were fighting for the good old Red White and Blue.

When they invaded the homeland of their enemy and the going got tough, they dug in and refused to yield to those who tried to drive them back into the sea.

With courage and the conviction that they were in the right this mighty army kept pushing towards their goal of freeing the enslaved people of the countries who had fallen victim to those who were trying to conquer the world.

The price was high and the battles long, but the determination of the free world never wavered in the face of seemingly overwhelming odds.

Way too many of our young men and women gave their lives in our fight for freedom, but not one of them will ever be forgotten as long as we who fought by their side are still alive.

On the home front, mothers, fathers, and sweethearts grieved the loss of their loved ones, they all shed tears when they received that dreaded telegram from the war department that told them of their loved ones demise. At the same time, they were proud to give of their own to keep this great country free.

Small flags with a star for each family member flew in the windows of those who had sons and daughters serving in the armed forces, they were displayed with much pride and many prayers were said for their loved ones who were serving in foreign lands around the world.

Now, years later, those of us who are still alive bow our heads in reverence to our fallen comrades, we still remember them as they were before that fragment of war tore into their body and their life ebbed away.

Our memories are still vivid and we recall the battles we fought those many, many years ago, or how we served in the non-combat units that rushed the much-needed supplies to the front lines. We all never faced the same conditions of war, but all were at war with our common enemies and did our duty as called.

With one common voice we stood fast and refused to succumb to the tyrants who were planning to split the spoils of war, we drove them back to the pits of hell from which they came.

We, the surviving comrades of those trying times are now dying at the rate of over one thousand a day; we are a dying breed, soldiers of old who proudly proclaim, "We did that which we had to do. We are proud to hand on to our children and their children's children a land free from the bondage of some foreign power."

One by one, we have turned the reins of power over to the next generation and assumed our rightful role of being the generation that freed the world from the likes of the axis powers.

Merrill Phillips

We still grieve our losses and pray for those who gave their all on our behalf. In our minds they will never die, they walk with us every day of our lives. The day fast approaches when we too will join them in death, a death they embraced so many, many years ago.

NATIONAL CEMETERIES

As I walk from grave to grave, I am inspired by the sacrifices that these brave men and women made on our behalf.

Otis McGee, William Lacy, Martin Lee, Scott Brown, Roland James, Robert Buck, to name a few who served so valiantly on the fields of battle around the world.

Some of these fallen comrades were fortunate enough to return home from war, but now lie in national cemeteries around the country.

Many carried the scars of battle to their grave, but never complained for they survived the hell of man killing man, the hell of prison camps, and untold torture.

While on the field of battle only the silence of death could blot out the cries of the wounded and dying, death was a relief to those who were ravaged by the weapons of war.

Their dues have been paid in this life, now is their time of rest, they hear no more roar of the cannon or the rattling of the machineguns.

They now lie in peace, free from the ravages of war, never again to face an enemy at home or abroad.

Jesus Christ now consoles their souls and has freed them from the burden of guilt of having to take another human life.

Peace is finally theirs; their ears hear only the voice of the great Shepherd as they gather around the throne of God.

Too few people visit them in their final resting place and thank them for giving of themselves so that we might remain free.

These now dead heroes were once the pride of their generation; let us not forget their sacrifices as through life we walk, these graves represent a once great fighting force of a free nation.

Through their unselfish efforts, we are free and will remain free as long as this nation has men and women like these to fight if necessary for our freedoms.

May these brave souls rest in peace in the presence of God and Jesus Christ, there they shall never more have to face an enemy on the field of battle.

Bless them dear Lord, keep them in your sheepfold and reward them for their unselfish deeds during the time of war.

Fallen comrades, you shall be remembered, you shall be honored, and your sacrifices shall never be forgotten as long as America remains a nation of the free and the brave.

May the stars and stripes forever wave over this great nation until the coming of Jesus Christ.

NEW THREAT TO OUR FREEDOM

We as a nation are going through a time in our history where we are facing a new threat to our freedoms. A threat from those who do not have any respect for human life and put themselves in a position of believing that they are doing God's work here on earth.

Most of the nations of the world condemn their acts of terrorism and will do whatever necessary to preserve the peaceful way of living that they have become used to through their own sacrifices.

By visiting a national cemetery and seeing the thousands of grave markers of those who have fought for our freedom ever since the birth of our nation is an inspiration to all who love freedom.

Many of those markers represent those who have given their lives on our behalf, never asking any personal favors from anyone so that their lives might be spared.

Everyone who has served in our armed forces knew from the moment of their enlistment that they faced the possibility of losing their lives in the defense of their country and yet they hesitated not to carry out their obligation to defend freedom wherever threatened.

Row upon row of grave markers are mute testimony of our love for freedom. If these honored men and women could speak to us of today they would tell us that if they had another chance to defend their country they would do so without reservations.

Many of those lying in our national cemeteries never faced combat; they did however contribute and sacrificed so that the frontline soldier could do his duty knowing that they had the support of their comrades in arms behind them.

As we fight against terrorism, keep in mind thoughts of those who fought for freedom before us and never allow ourselves to become complacent and say, "Let someone else do it." It is the duty of all of us to come together and stand as a nation as we have done so many times before.

As many faults we have as a nation we are still the only nation who has the will power to aggressively seek out those who are bent on terrorizing the rest of the world and do something about it, for sooner or later they will strike us.

Listen to the voices of the past and know that our future can only be secure when we come together with one voice and stand as a symbol to the world that our nation will never bow or succumb to those who wish to destroy our way of life.

The fighting men and women of the past secured our future and now it is time for us to secure the future of generations yet unborn.

It will be a constant struggle and commitment on the part of all of us to see to it that terrorism will never get a stronghold on our way of life.

Remembering the past and honoring those who sacrificed their lives on our behalf will give us the courage to face our future with the same determination to defend our freedom as they defended theirs.

Listen to the voices on the wind and you will hear the cries for freedom from time immemorial. It is you and I who has to keep the fires of freedom burning brightly so that the oppressed nations of the world will have the same courage to keep striving for their own freedom.

No oppressor will ever reign long (although at the time it may seem long) enough to stamp out the fires of freedom that burns so bright in the hearts of those who have a desire for it, and have the will to fight and die for it.

Terrorism is just another means by which one nation or organization uses to destroy that which they do not understand. They have been lead astray by the evil of the world and it may be necessary to destroy the means by which they carry out their terrorist acts in order to restore peace.

As we as a nation have defeated our enemies in the past and then helped them to rebuild a peaceful community, so must we do now.

To turn an enemy into a viable friend is a formable task, but we have done it before and we can do it again. An enemy is nothing more than a misguided friend who for a while lost their way.

Keep the picture of struggling men and women who faced death every day while defending our freedoms and strive to understand and love those who live and think differently than we do in our prayers and thoughts, for once we too was a rogue nation fighting for what we believed in.

We as a nation have been blessed and so must we share our blessings with other nations.

OLD GLORY

Wrap yourself in the flag of U.S.A., let not one drop
of her blood be spilt in vain.

Long may Old Glory wave over the home of the free
and the brave.

From the rising of the sun to the setting of the moon,
let freedom ring from the mountains to the sea.

May the stars and stripes wave during the darkest
of nights and light up the heavens so bright.

When it rains may the seeds of freedom sprout
forth across the land of the free.

Let the trumpets of freedom resound from Mexico to
the Canadian border, from sea to shining sea.

Let news of freedom flow from Washington D.C. that
will set all hearts aglow.

Wrap yourself in the good old Red, White, and Blue,
resist oppression and live free.

From youth to the aged and all in between, stand fast
with Old Glory waving in your hand.

Hold that banner high that represents the U.S. of A.,
let not the oppressors of the world trample on
Old Glory and desecrate her name.

Stand fast and rejoice as Old Glory waves over the
home of the brave and the land of the free.

May Old Glory forever be a symbol that represents
man's fight for freedom and a place where he
can live free.

THE OLD RED, WHITE AND BLUE

Many of us have witnessed and participated in our nation's struggle to maintain our freedom, to you I dedicate the following piece about our flag that we so proudly call, THE OLD RED, WHITE, AND BLUE.

First, I would like to remind you of some of the struggles that we have gone through in our lifetime.

From the battlefields of the Pacific, Europe, Africa, the middle and Far East, Old Glory has been tattered and torn by shellfire, but was never lowered in defeat. Sometimes battles were lost and Old Glory was ground in the dust of the earth, only to rise again to let the world know that the Red, White, and the Blue was triumphant over her foes.

The Red, White, and Blue is the symbol of our nation and as long as we hold the truths of God foremost in our hearts and minds the Red, White, and Blue will never have to be lowered in defeat. We have rallied around our flag ever since we have been a nation. Even our enemies respect our flag and know wherever they see her flying over a field of battle she will never bow or succumb to tyranny.

There is only one symbol greater than the Red, White, and Blue and that is the cross upon which our Lord and Savior, Jesus Christ, gave His life so that we as His followers might be free from the bondage of sin and have eternal life.

To these two great symbols we dedicate our lives and strive to uphold what they stand for, knowing that one day we have to answer to God as to how we conducted ourselves while living here on earth.

Admiral Yamo Moto of the Japanese navy put it best when after attacking Pearl Harbor at the start of World War11 he said, "I believe we have just awakened a great sleeping giant.", and how true that turned out to be.

Only under the auspices of God can such a flag and freedom loving nation survive, for God is the very basis upon which our freedoms are based.

The next time you see the Red, White, and Blue unfurl in the breezes of freedom, stop, place your hand over your heart and pay reverence to those who fought for and those who gave their lives for the cause of freedom.

THE GRAND OLD FLAG

Keep our Grand Old Flag flying high over the land of the free and the brave; keep her flying high, whether at home or overseas.

Too many of our youth have given their lives to assure freedom for all who dwell in this great land to allow the Grand Old Flag to be desecrated or burned before our eyes.

May our national leaders stand as examples of men and women of freedom to a war torn world, with resolve in their hearts to always stand for freedom under God as their moral guide.

Whenever called upon to defend freedom beyond our shores respect the flag that has flown from our conception as a nation, honor our nation by being ambassadors of freedom, fight for freedom rather than for dominance and gain.

As we struggled as a growing nation and fought against foreign powers, so help those who long for freedom from oppression and when victory is achieved return to our shores until once again we are called upon to help.

We as a free nation have an obligation to help to spread freedom to all who seek freedom and ask for our help, do so under the Grand Old Flag that represents our struggle to gain and maintain our freedom.

A flag represents the feelings of a nation, in our case the Grand Old Flag is a national treasure, one worth defending at all costs.

Many nations of this divided world despise us and will do their best to keep freedom in check, their leaders hold to a different ideology and govern without consideration of what their constituents want, when opposed they hesitate not to use strong arm tactics to maintain control.

Be adamant and tenacious, do not allow anyone to desecrate the Grand Old Flag in the name of freedom of speech, desecrating the Grand Old Flag should bring outrage from all freedom loving people; freedom has its obligations, one of which is to hold the Grand Old Flag to a higher moral standard, one befitting us as a free nation.

Just because we are a free nation does not give any of us the right to desecrate the lives of those who gave their all so that we can remain free. Desecrating these lives desecrates the Grand Old Flag and this cannot be tolerated if we are to remain a leading nation of the world.

The Grand Old Flag came out of our struggle for freedom and each stitch in this Grand Old Flag represents a fallen hero who thought enough of our nation to put his or her life on the line in defense of the Grand Old Flag and a better way of life.

Not a perfect life by no stretch of the imagination, but a life that has kept us a free nation rallying around a flag that we hold dear to our hearts and a willingness to defend it against all who try to tear us down and destroy our way of living.

World war11 was the greatest example of a nation rallying around a flag and defending it against all odds. Looking back on those times, we came together as a people and disregarded the odds and fought on and never looked back until we concluded the war in victory. The Grand Old Flag inspired us all to do that which we had to do.

We can be proud of our nation and hold the Grand Old Flag as our rallying point when threatened by some foreign power. The Grand Old Flag is a special flag and will remain so as long as there are those who will step forward and defend it regardless of the price.

With the Grand Old Flag in one hand and the Bible in the other, this nation can withstand the onslaught of tyranny throughout the world and be an example to all who are seeking freedom from oppression.

WORLD WAR11

We of the World War11 generation will never forget the struggle our country went through, some on the home front, others on the battlefields of the world, stretched to our limits we sacrificed many of our pleasures to contribute to the war effort.

Rationing became a way of life; we gave so the soldiers on the frontline could have the materials that they needed to carry the war to the enemy. We regretted not these sacrifices, for our way of life and freedom had been attacked by ruthless forces that were hell bent on destroying not only our way of life, but the very country in which we lived.

We younger World War11 veterans were still in school when the war broke out; we were inspired by the acts of bravery and heroism that was coming from the frontlines. We studied hard and prayed that the war would come to an end before it became our time to join the ranks of the armed forces, but this was not to be. One by one, we joined our fighting brothers in whatever capacity we qualified.

Schooled in our chosen service we ventured forth and faced the greatest foe the world had ever known up to that time, never once was it a given that we as a nation would survive this world struggle between good and evil.

The Merchant Marines was an entity unto itself, these brave men put their lives on the line as ones who ran our great merchant fleet without being recognized as a fighting force. Without them, the war could not have been carried to the enemy on their own soil. They suffered death and the threat of death upon the high seas. Many gave their lives at sea when attacked by a relentless enemy submarine force.

We prayed a lot and never allowed defeat after defeat discourage us or deter us in our endeavor to turn the tide of battle in our favor. In this endeavor, thousands upon thousands of our youths gave their lives so that we as a nation could survive, never asking to be relieved from the task that was before them. They knew that many of their comrades would not survive the battles that faced them and yet they stood fast during some of the fiercest battles ever fought.

The hearts of families all over the nation were broken time after time when they received the dreaded news that their son or daughter had given their all in the defense of their country. These were times of national mourning and yet the men and women on the home front never lost hope of eventually becoming victorious in their struggle for freedom, everyone stuck to their guns and kept the materials of war flowing to those who were on the frontline.

Though these losses were hard to take, they only deepened our resolve that our nation could survive against the onslaught of those who wanted to rule the world. There were times when we had doubts, times that tested our faith and times that strengthened our faith, times to join hands with our neighbors and work as a nation to bring peace to our shores.

Freedom has its price, unfortunately it is the youth of our nation who have to bear the brunt of our conflicts, have to sacrifice their lives so that the rest of us can enjoy the freedom that our forefathers fought and died for. Our youth forms the backbone of our fighting forces and are to be honored for keeping us free.

We who were once of that younger generation, veterans of previous wars relinquish our day in the sun to you younger fighting men and women who are now serving our nation. We regret that you still have to go to war, but as long as there are those who want to see this nation defeated then we of the past pass on to you the flag of freedom to carry to victory as we once did.

Think not that your sacrifices go unnoticed; our hearts are saddened because we (the older veterans) have been where you are now. We are inspired by your courage and willingness to defend our nation whenever and wherever our freedom is threatened.

Your sacrifices will enable generations yet to be born to live in a free nation and the day will come when you will hand on to them the responsibilities that we handed on to you. The quest for freedom requires that every generation be vigilant and forth coming in the struggle to remain free.

A PRAYER FOR OUR
AGED VETERANS

Holy Father, one at a time we the ageing veterans join our comrades in arms in death and lie in sacred ground until the second coming of Jesus Christ.

Many died on the field of battle and were buried on foreign soil. Though far from their native land they now rest in peace. Others were fortunate to survive the hell of battle and returned home to marry and raise a new generation. One that will take our place on the field of battle when called upon. Even others were maimed and scared for life as the bullets ravaged their bodies and left them dependent upon others.

The more fortunate veterans never saw combat and yet without them none of the combat veterans would have survived to return home. Their duty was to see to it the materials of war reached the front lines at all costs. One could not survive without the other. We were all part of a mighty fighting force that defended our country both at home and abroad.

No one command was superior to another, for without all commands working together could we as a nation survive. There was no doubt rivalry between units, but when it came to supporting one another under combat conditions or getting a job done all rivalry was put aside until the mission was completed.

The burial of any veteran is a solemn occasion, Day by day veteran after veteran is laid to rest, and death relieves them of the horrors of war that they carried to their graves. No longer do they smell the stench of death on the field of battle or hear the cries of the wounded, finally they are at peace.

It is with humble pride that we the living veterans gather together to celebrate the lives of these valiant men and women. We shed silent tears of gratitude for their contribution to the freedom that we the living enjoy.

It is without a doubt the greatest unselfish act that anyone can do to defend their country in its times of need. Not only defend their country, but also be willing to give their lives so that the rest of us might live free. No greater sacrifice could be asked of anyone.

Is it not the duty of everyone to do all that they can to see to it that all veterans are given the gratitude of a grateful nation, without exception? Join a grateful nation in paying homage to the veterans who fought so gallantly and gave so much so that this nation might remain free and our democratic form of government might survive against all odds.

UNDER THE WEEPING WILLOW

Beneath the weeping willow tree is a grave marker with the inscription "Unknown Soldier", unknown to all but God.

Its branches reach to the ground; they shed tears of sorrow for the family who will never again see one of their own.

The weeping willows roots run deep and embrace the coffin of the "Unknown Soldier".

This brave soul now enjoys the promise of God, to keep him now and forevermore safe from all harm.

The day that he died he never knew when the end came, he left his earthly home and stepped into the presence of God, never again to die or be alone.

Whether he died many wars ago or yesterday in the defense of his home, the weeping willow weeps on for the "Unknown Soldier".

The "Unknown Soldier" grave markers represent valiant men and women who gave their all in defense of their native land.

The "Unknown Soldier" now marches to a different voice, a voice unheard by those whom he left behind.

We the living owe our freedom to the sacrifices of these unknown warriors.

They now rest in peace far from the battlefields where they gave their all so that you and I might be free.

THOSE WHO SERVED

Those who served during the hell of World War11 are fortunate indeed or are they, for they carry within them the memories of those who lost their lives in the struggle for freedom.

They will carry with them to their graves the horror of war, of those who were captured, tortured and died while held in enemy prison of war camps or those who died in combat or the results of combat.

All of this may have taken place well over sixty years ago, but those who served in the armed forces at that time will remember it the rest of their lives and when called to mind will seem as only yesterday.

Tears will roll down the checks of those who survived that hell on earth, when memories of their fallen comrades come to mind, but at the time, survival was foremost in their minds.

Not all veterans served in combat rolls, but all who served were in danger of being killed at any given moment. Death was an ever present companion to all who took up the cause of freedom, whether at home or abroad.

We were but young boys and girls who were caught up in a war not of our making, many of us volunteered in order to serve in the unit of our choice, others were drafted and served where appointed.

No one thought that it would be they who would die because of enemy firepower, but in the mind of all of us the constant danger of being the next one to die for the cause of freedom.

Many civilians on both sides lost their lives due to and the results of combat, no one was exempt from that stray bullet or bomb that fell on the cities and countryside of those nations who were directly involved in the combat zones of that day.

Millions of combat troops and civilians died because of the desires of just three men with the ambition of ruling the world. Truly, a classic example of evil against good, only by the grace of God did good overcome evil.

Today when someone comes up to a veteran of World War11 and pats them on their back and says, "Thank you for your service to our country." Is like taking credit for something that we had no control over, we were called to serve and we did. We did what we had to do.

To the veteran the real heroes are those who gave their lives for the cause of freedom, we, the living were fortunate to survive the rolls we played in a world conflict, the memories of our fallen comrades will be with us until we too join them in death.

To have lived through that period of history was truly an event in our lives that will be with us for the rest of our days, our memories of that period of history will never fade and an experience that we would never wish upon anyone. The carnage of war cannot be fully known until one is caught up in it.

To talk with many of the young people of today and realize that they do not have a clue what the veterans of World War11 went through during their war years is disheartening indeed.

It is sad to realize that the younger generations do not appreciate what their ancestors went through so that they of today can reap the bounty of today without concern for those who fought and died so many years ago.

Unless this changes those of today will one day have to go through of what we of the older generation went through when we were young, for without the knowledge of the mistakes made before and during world conflict, history will repeat itself.

If another world conflict were to repeat itself, many of us older, veterans would be among the first to volunteer for combat, or at least in mind and soul. Our bodies could not stand the rigors of war again, but to protect our grandchildren and great-grandchildren we would try.

No veteran would wish the hell of war on anyone in this country or any other country, for no one is a victor, oh yes, someone wins and someone losses, but in the end all are losers, lives are changed forever during times of conflict. No one escapes wars without scars; scars that never really heal in the minds of those who witness the death of those who die way too young in foreign lands that they did not know existed before facing them in a combat situation.

As it has been so aptly said, "War is hell." something to be avoided if possible. Ask any veteran of any war if he or she would advocate war as a means of settling differences between nations and I assure you the answer would be a resounding NO.

SADLY SOME MUST DIE FOR THE CAUSE OF FREEDOM

As long as we live in this world there will be war, wars that rob families of their young men and women to die in the fight for freedom. Not only freedom for ourselves but also freedom for all freedom loving people of the world.

Whether these peace loving people are from our country or some country half way around the world, they are all seeking peace for themselves and generations yet to be born. In the process, it is inevitable that some must die for the cause; this is the nature of war.

Wars are unavoidable as long as two nations cannot come to terms with each other's ideologies; it has been this way since the beginning of time and will continue until the second coming of Jesus Christ.

During every conflict, there are those who oppose war and make those who try to help others to find freedom from oppression look like war mongers, mostly these are the ones who want freedom and live free without having to participate in fighting for freedom.

Then there are those who will go to war at the drop of a hat, these look forward to the profits of war that they can put in their pockets, growing wealthy from another's sacrifice and misfortune.

These same people like living in a country where there hasn't been a conflict in their backyard for a long time and have no experience of having their neighbors and families marched off to some concentration camp and there slaughtered just because they are different then themselves.

In our present struggle against terrorism and carrying, the war to the heart of terrorist activities has divided our nation, some willing to take our hits on our soil and not pursue freedom from terrorism through carrying the fight to the homeland of the terrorist.

Others believe is stamping out terrorism no matter where it occurs, on our soil or the soil of some foreign country, to be a friend and ally to those who sacrifice every day in the pursuit of personal freedom, to them it is a noble cause.

All who have the desire to be free from terrorism or any other form of war have to make the decision of whether they want freedom enough to fight for it or compromise with those who are bent of destroying all who oppose their ideologies, freedom without willing to fight for it is a hollow freedom indeed.

We are our brother's keeper and as such, it behooves us to step forward and help our neighbors to obtain freedom. One day we might just be in the situation where we will need the help of others to regain or preserve our own freedom, no nation is an island unto itself.

To yield to an oppressive regime and condone their actions as long as it is not in our backyard is surrendering our freedom in exchange for not standing up to those who want to see our way of life destroyed.

To do nothing but talk encourages evil to spread its lies and influence around the world. Doing nothing to stem evil is just another way of saying that we do not care what you do as long as you leave us alone. Those who can live with this scenario can tear a nation apart more than war itself.

Freedom, no matter where it is pursued comes with a price. Our fighting forces realize this more than the public and yet our fighting forces step forward and offer their lives so that others may obtain what we now enjoy, freedom from oppression and terrorism.

The public is not privileged to the information that the military has, therefore the public draws a different conclusions of whether we should stand up to terrorism or just let them go about their business of destroying freedom loving people around the world. Perhaps the public should know more, it might open their eyes to what is really going on and how ruthless terrorist really are.

Life is meaningless to the terrorist as long as they obtain their objectives; those who can send their own young children into a crowded market or meeting place and blow themselves up in the name of their god certainly would not hesitate to kill you and me, just because we do not believe as they do.

To turn from or condone terrorism is aiding and abetting the enemy of freedom, freedom given to us by God. We have to choose between freedom or surrendering to those who everyday blow themselves up trying to rid the world of freedom loving people, Freedom from terrorism is a worldwide struggle and must be seen and acted upon from that perspective.

War against freedom is the only means by which terrorist can advance their agenda and they will continue to push their agenda upon all who oppose them. Force is the only thing they understand, it will be a long hard struggle, but the freedom loving people of the world can and will defeat terrorism as long as they stick together and form a common fighting force against the evil of this world.

OLD GLORY STILL FLIES OVER THE LAND OF THE FREE AND THE BRAVE

If it wasn't for the bravery and gallant effort of these now deceased veterans this land of the free and brave might be under the rule of some foreign aggressor.

The hallowed grounds of our national cemeteries are being filled with the remains of our fighting men and women way too fast.

They lie as mute testimony of the willingness of ordinary men and women to answer the call of their nation to defend itself against tyranny, both domestic and foreign.

One cannot visit the resting place of these devoted men and women without having a feeling of gratitude and saying a prayer of thanks.

As I sit here and witness the burial of a fellow comrade in arms I thank God for allowing me to live in a country where if called upon its citizenry is willing to defend their freedom at all costs.

May the flag of our great nation continue to inspire generations yet unborn to defend if necessary this land of freedom in which we life.

May the blood stained flags of the past encourage us of the present generation and generations to come to step forward and be counted whenever our freedom is threatened.

Not all nations of the world have the freedom that our veterans have given their time and lives for.

Their shed blood should be a reminder that freedom comes with a price and that freedom is a reward for defending our nation against all aggressors.

Freedom should not be taken for granted; we can lose it if we as a nation become complacent and refuse to help other nations to go through what we have already gone through.

The struggle for freedom should be the concern of all patriotic citizens, whether of this nation or other nations.

God has granted us of the United States of America a special place in this world. To stand strong and be willing to defend freedom both at home and abroad.

No one nation can stand alone against the tyranny of the world. We as a free nation must stand as an example that the love of God and the love of freedom can prevail if its citizenry is willing lay down their lives in the defense thereof.

Without the freedom that we now enjoy we would be just another nation struggling to survive.

The veterans who now lay in peace represent our nation's youth who would rather die fighting for freedom than be enslaved by some foreign power.

With Old Glory flying high in the breezes of freedom, this nation shall survive as long as its citizens put God, country, and love of freedom before themselves.

STILL FREE

It was for the love and respect for freedom that we have gone to war against those powers that wanted to silence freedom around the world.

Many of the youth of our nation have sacrificed their lives so that the rest of us might remain free.

They died on battlefields scattered around the world so that we here in America would not have to face the hell of war on our home soil.

They hesitated not to do whatever was necessary to defend this great land that bore them.

In the giving of their lives, they were freed from hell on earth and now reside in the presence of God.

It is only fitting that we honor our fallen comrades and in so doing we honor the freedom that they died for.

Freedom is the one thing the youth of our nation will come together for and defend at all costs.

Freedom taken for granted is not true freedom unless we are willing to sacrifice all that we have for it, even our lives.

It seems that every few years we are called upon to defend freedom somewhere in this imperfect world.

Satan is always at work trying to pit nation against nation in an effort to spread his influence around the world.

Fortunately, there are enough freedom loving people in this world to offset those who have the desired to rule the world by force.

It is with great pride and humility that we come together to honor our fallen veterans and living veterans for putting their lives on the line for the cause of freedom.

During World War11, they came forth from all walks of life and formed the greatest fighting force that the world has ever seen.

With the flag of freedom flying before them, they defeated all who would come between them and freedom. Just the word freedom brings out the best in all of us.

The more freedom was threatened the more our country came together to defend freedom.

This great nation of America was conceived and born out of an attempt to depress freedom and make us bend to the will of a totalitarian form of government.

We took the bit of freedom in our mouth and never gave up until we were free. Over the years, we have defended our freedoms in whatever way was necessary to remain free.

During World War11, we as a nation called upon our youth to defend us to the last man if necessary. Out of this movement came the greatest generation that we as a nation have witnessed. To have this generation pass without acknowledging what they fought and gave their lives for would be a travesty.

It is time and fitting that we honor these freedom loving men and women by erecting a memorial to their honor so that future generations do not forget that the freedoms that they enjoy came with a price that we the veterans sacrificed so much for.

It is the veterans of all wars who understand what it means to go to war with the anticipation of giving their lives in the defense of freedom if necessary.

Join the ranks of those who through war and peace are ready, willing, and able to step forth whenever called upon to protect this great nation from aggression.

Let freedom ring throughout the world from the mountains to the sea, may those who seek freedom find it before this world they leave. Let those who have found freedom help those who are seeking freedom, for it is God's will that all be free.

THE UNKNOWN SOLDIER

Among the sea of headstones in our national cemeteries with name, rank, division of service, date of birth and date of death are the headstones of the "Unknown Soldier". They fan out to form rows as if they were in marching formation.

They differ from the rest of the grave markers in respect that they have no name, rank, or division of service, nor do they have the date of birth or death, just the inscription, "Unknown Soldier".

These are the men who entered battle and never returned. They lost their identity fighting for freedom, fighting to keep our nation free from foreign oppression.

They were men just like you and me, with loved ones waiting for their return. They died in heat of battle and never heard the shell that burst and took their identity away; their lives cut short by the horrors of war.

U—Unknown by all except God.

N—Never returned home to know the love of a wife or raise a family.

K—Know no more suffering or pain, just the love of God.

N—Never again will they hear the cry of the wounded or feel the sting of death.

O—Only they know the true cost of war.

W—Would do it over again to keep their country free.

N—Never again will they have to face the horrors of war.

S—Safe in the arms of almighty God.

O—Only after death were they free from the hell of war.

L—Like generations before they faced their enemies and gave their all so their loved ones could live free.

D—Death came all too soon for these brave and courageous men.

I—In the heat of battle they stood their ground unto death.

E—Entered into the kingdom of God with their head held high.

R—Ready and willing to give their lives to keep their country free.

As long as there are wars, there will be those who give their all and come home unknown to their fellowman.

O merciful God, comfort these "Unknown Soldiers", grant them peace, and let not their sacrifices be in vain.

THIS GREAT LAND
CALLED AMERICA

Governments have come and gone, America was formed in the hearts of our founding fathers with the laws of God on their minds.

God guided our founding fathers to form a government controlled by the vote of the common man.

God intended this newly formed government to be an example for all nations to follow.

Freedom from oppression was one of the building blocks that formed the foundation of this great nation.

This nation like no other nation on earth depended upon God to direct our founding fathers in forming a government that has never been equaled.

The might and power of America comes from the right hand of God.

Merrill Phillips

From sea to sea, from mountain to vale the people of this land joined together in protecting and upholding the constitution that forms the fabric of our society.

Great are her sons and daughters who have fought and died so that America can stand as a nation among nations guided by the hand of God.

To those who wish to destroy or subdue our God given rights have no place in this great country; they shall be removed by their own hand.

Christians raise your voices and stand united against the foes of iniquity, praise God and give Him credit for giving you and me the opportunity to live in a land where all people are equal and free.

America is the greatest experiment in a democratic form of government in the history of man, to see if the common people can stand as one and control their own destiny.

For every star that has been added to our flag represents a new state, formed to govern itself within the context of the wishes of our founding fathers.

America gives hope to all of the deprived people the world around, and offers proof that a nation can be free from tyrannical governments and prosper.

The cry for freedom will be heard throughout time, as a nation America has the opportunity to set an example for other founding nations to follow.

With God at the helm of state America will remain free and provide a place where freedom loving people of the world can come and prosper.

God has blessed America, without God America would not be.